The Greedies

WRITTEN BY JUDY KAMPIA
ILLUSTRATED BY GREGORY SNADER

To order additional copies of this book, contact:
Xlibris Corporation
1-888-795-4274
www.Xlibris.com
Orders@Xlibris.com

In a building called Forgotten Manors, on Allmine Avenue, lives the Greedy family. The Greedies have five children. One boy is named Speedy Greedy. He always hurries to be first at everything. Feedy Greedy is his younger sister. She does not care if Speedy is first, as long as she gets the most. Sometimes Feedy eats more than she really wants just to be sure no one else has more. Speedy and Feedy have a sister named Needy Greedy. She thinks she needs whatever someone else has. But since Needy will not help herself, she whines and begs for someone else to give her what she wants. The oldest brother in the family is named Indeed Greedy. He is indeed very greedy. Indeed always wants the best and biggest for himself.

There is one child in the family who is different. Her name is Not. Little Not Greedy is a polite child. She patiently waits her turn and shares whatever she has.

One summer day, the Greedy children were having a typical breakfast of spilled juice, flying rice cereal, and stomachaches. Speedy had eaten too fast, Feedy had eaten too much, and Needy had eaten while screaming.

After breakfast, Mom took the little Greedies to the grocery store. As usual, Needy asked for everything she saw or did not see. "Gimme some Frosted Frinkles like we see on TV!" she demanded. "I need an artichoke! Why don't we ever get cantaloupe soda-pop? I need those chocolate-covered carrots!"

"And I want some peace and quiet!" said Mom. "Needy, go sit in the car!"

Feedy went ahead down the aisle to pick out what she wanted. She was carrying a large plastic bottle of soda-pop, three jars of marshmallow cream, and two boxes of caramel corn. When she reached for a giant-sized box of doughnuts, everything else slipped to the floor. The soda-pop floated down the aisle while the marshmallow cream glued the caramel corn to the floor. Feedy felt afraid, so she snuck out to the car with Needy.

Meanwhile, Speedy raced down the aisle trying to be the first one to choose breakfast cereal. He wanted to be sure Mom got only the kind he liked. As he ran, he knocked over two gallons of bleach, bumped a cart into a stack of coconuts, and tripped into a tray of slimy fresh fish. As fish and coconuts crashed to the floor, goo spattered in all directions, causing Speedy to slip and fall on his bottom. When he tried to get up, he saw above him a very large man in a white apron. Pointing his arm in the air, the man shouted only one word--"OUT!" Speedy ran to the car. But his sisters would not let him in because he smelled like fish.

Indeed Greedy had been following to make sure Speedy did not get more of anything than he did. As Indeed ran, he slipped on the spilled soda pop and fell face-first onto the marshmallow cream, which made the caramel corn stick to his face. Then he saw the manager coming towards him and stepped backwards. Indeed slipped, bottom first, into the bleach, which turned the back of his blue jeans white. When he returned to the car, the others asked, "Indeed, why do you have brown bumps on your face and a white seat in your new jeans?

Little Not Greedy remained with Mom. She enjoyed looking at all the new products, but did not touch them. After she and Mom went through the checkout counter, the clerk handed her a large lollipop. She explained, "We are giving these to all the children who come through the line as part of our anniversary sale."

"Thank you very much," smiled Not, licking the lollipop.

When the little Greedies came home, they decided to watch television. "Me first!" shouted Speedy as he rushed to turn on the TV.

"I need to watch a game show to see what new things I'd like to have," whined Needy.

"No!" demanded Feedy, "Let's see if *The Chubby Chef* is on!"

"No! It's time for *Monsters on Planet Q*" argued Indeed, grabbing the remote control. But Speedy was pressing the channel buttons on the TV at the same time. Speedy and Indeed rapidly switched buttons back and forth until the television was stuck on channel 14. A talk show host introduced his guest, who would discuss the dangers of too much TV for children.

"Change the channel! Change the channel!" chanted Needy and Feedy. Little Not left them to read a book.

Not Greedy read until the doorbell rang. It was Rich, who lived on the next street in a huge house with a big pool. Greeting little Not, he asked: "It's so hot! How'd you like to come over for a swim?"

"Sure, as soon as I ask my mom," exclaimed Not. "Thanks!" Then she went upstairs to find Mom and a bathing suit.

"We're coming too." said Speedy, Feedy, Needy and Indeed.

"Sorry," said Rich. "My Mom says the rest of you are too much trouble--even dangerous! Speedy always wants to be first. So he runs and slips on the wet pavement and knocks other kids down. Feedy keeps asking for snacks. Needy whines for all the water toys and all the attention. And Indeed won't let the rest of us on the diving board. My Mom says only Not is allowed to come."

So only Not spent that hot morning in the pool with Rich.

When Not came home, the little Greedies had lunch. "Me first!" shouted Speedy. As he ran to the table, he tripped over the wind-up toy gorilla Needy had been too lazy to put away. He landed with his face in the butter.

"I wanted the butter!" cried Needy. Then she added, "Pass the bread! Where are the crackers? I wanted chocolate milk instead of cola!"

Meanwhile, Indeed lined all five glasses of cola in a row to see which had the most. While he switched around the glasses, Feedy reached across the table for the hot dogs. But as she grabbed them, she knocked over the entire row of glasses spilling cola and ice right into Indeed's lap.

"I want more cola!" screamed Needy.

"Gimme the most!" insisted Feedy.

"Me first!" demanded Speedy.

"This is cold!" shivered Indeed.

"There is no more cola," Mom explained. "I'll bring you all milk instead."

"Me first!" shouted Speedy, and he drank his milk fast enough to get the hiccups. Needy still argued for chocolate milk. Indeed poured himself *three* full glasses. Seeing this, Feedy did not want anyone to have more than she did. So she drank *four* full glasses of milk and could not stop burping. Her stomach was so full from four glasses of milk and seven hot dogs that every time she burped, another button flew off her shirt. Everyone laughed except Needy, who was still asking for pickled pumpkin relish on her hot dog. Then she noticed that there *were* no more hot dogs. Everyone stopped laughing and complained that Feedy had eaten all the hot dogs. So Mom made grilled-cheese sandwiches.

"Me...hic...first...hic" hiccupped Speedy. He put the first sandwich into his mouth so quickly, and burnt his tongue so badly on the melted cheese, that he could not say, "Me first!" for an hour.

"I...burp...want the... biggest," burped Feedy. Then Indeed looked through the stack of sandwiches for one that was neither too dark nor too light, and Needy complained that they were *all* too dark or too light.

9

Poor Not! She waited patiently for the food to be passed, but it never came. Now there was nothing left for her. Then Mom walked in with Brenda Berger. "Oh, I see you've already eaten," sighed Brenda with disappointment. "I was hoping to see Not before lunch so that I could invite her to eat at Dad's place with me." Brenda's father owned the town's most popular restaurant, Berger's Burgers, which served delicious fries, hamburgers and shakes in booths shaped like little carriages. Brenda continued: "Dad just called to say that Bippy the Clown was visiting the restaurant today and passing out prizes. He said I could treat a friend."

"Oh, I haven't eaten yet," explained Not, "only the others have."

"I wouldn't invite them anyway," laughed Brenda. The last time your family came, Speedy ran around filling his pockets with extra straws. Needy kept whining for things we did not serve. Feedy and Indeed got into a fight over who had the most fries. Dad hopes they never come back. But I'm glad you can come, Not--your the friend I picked."

10

When Not returned from Berger's Burgers, she had five helium balloons the clown had given her. "Look, I have something to share!" she told the other Greedies.

"Me first!" shouted Speedy. But he grabbed so quickly that he did not have a tight grip on the string, and the balloon escaped into the air.

"I want that one!" Indeed yelled, taking the biggest balloon. But he did not realize that the biggest one had a tiny hole. Soon it leaked into a mere piece of rubber.

"Gimme the prettiest one," commanded Feedy. But she had just been eating pecan pie and had a fork in her hand. When she reached for the balloon, her fork popped it.

"I'd rather have an orange balloon, with purple dots," whined Needy, "Go ask that clown if he has one!"

When Not refused, Needy agreed to take a pink balloon, but insisted that it be tossed to her as she sat in her chair. Since Needy was too lazy to run for it, her balloon also disappeared into the air.

11

"Oh, well, we can all play with my balloon," Not suggested. "But let's play indoors where it won't fly away."

"I'll throw first," Speedy reminded the others. He threw the balloon while Not and Indeed tried to catch it. Feedy was too full to run for it, and Needy remained in her chair demanding that the others give it to her.

Then Indeed, greediest of all, laughed, "Ha! Now I've got the balloon, and I'm going to keep it!" He sat in a corner tightly clutching the balloon. But he wondered why he was not having any fun. He could not think of a thing to do with a balloon all by himself.

Not just shook her head and looked out the window. She noticed her friend, Lotta, approaching with her mother, Mrs. Phunn. Not invited them in. "We wanted to ask you to come with us to see a movie at the mall cinema. We're on our way right now." said Lotta.

"I want to go too," whined Needy, stamping her feet.

"Me first!" interrupted Speedy.

"I want three bags of popcorn," Feedy demanded.

""Let's go!" shouted Indeed as he pushed the others away.

"No Indeed!" Mrs. Phunn replied. "The last time we took all of you, we were asked to leave early. Speedy ran down the aisle trying to be first, Indeed pushed other children out of the way to get the seat he wanted, and Feedy ate everyone's popcorn. Then Needy disturbed the audience with constant complaining. We are only inviting Not this time."

"Thank you for inviting me," said Not. She waved good-bye to her brothers and sisters and thanked Mom for letting her go.

Not came home in time for supper. After supper, Mrs. Greedy told the little Greedies to get ready for bed. Since Feedy had eaten way too much again, her pajamas split down the middle. Then Needy shouted, "I need my orange polka-dot pajamas. Gimme milk and cake first! Where is my cuddly stuffed red iguana? I can't sleep without it!"

"I get the bathroom first!" insisted Speedy, running ahead of the others.

"Wait...wait," Feedy said faintly, "I feel kinda sick" (Her nine pieces of chicken, three tomatoes, two bags of corn chips with salsa, five pickles, and two bowls of blackberry ice cream, had not mixed well in her stomach.)

"No, I'm first," said Speedy, pushing her back.

Feedy followed closely behind mumbling, "But..but...b...b...uh...uh...uh, ugh...ggg."

Speedy was first to the bathroom, but he made Feedy wait so long that her giant supper came back up---all over his shoes.

After rinsing off his shoes, Speedy rushed for the toothpaste. Indeed grabbed it at the same time. While the boys struggled with the tube, Needy was screaming: "I want the tooth paste. Gimme the tooth paste!" Just then, the boys squeezed the tube together so hard that the toothpaste squirted across the room--right into Needy's hollering mouth!

"Well, now she has her tooth paste!" laughed Indeed. But as he looked down, he saw that the tube was empty. So Mom made the boys use Dad's toothpaste, which smelled like the dentist's office.

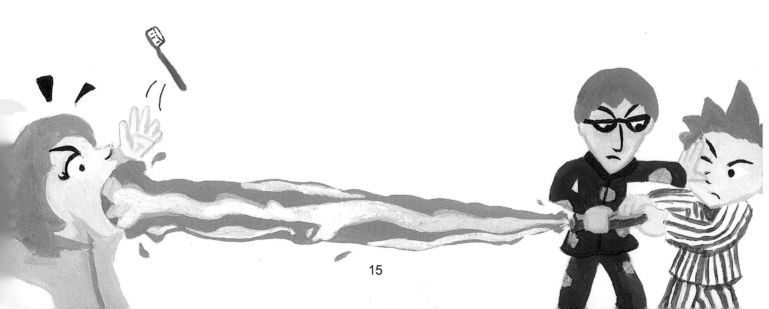

Thinking that at least he could be first in bed, Speedy ran and pounced onto the big bed he shared with Indeed. But he jumped so hard that the bed collapsed. While Speedy tried to fix it, Indeed climbed into the slanted bed and wrapped the blanket tightly around himself. He was not comfortable this way, but he would rather be uncomfortable than share the blanket.

Eventually Speedy realized that he could not fix the bed and climbed in. "Gimme some covers!" he yelled, trying to yank the blanket away. But Indeed yanked back. The boys pulled the blanket back and forth, each time pulling harder. On the thirty-seventh yank, it split down the middle. Tired from pulling, each boy took his half and fell asleep on the broken bed.

In the girls' room Feedy wrapped all the blankets tightly around herself. Needy began to cry, "I want my covers! I want my covers! Gimme! Gimme! Gimme!" The more Needy kicked and cried, the more Feedy did not want to share. Finally they fell asleep. Needy was too cool, and would wake up with a cold. Feedy was too warm, and would wake up with a rash.

Meanwhile, Not had fallen asleep in a cozy sleeping bag. She slept peacefully inside a small tent near a campfire. Her friend Dot had invited her to spend the weekend on a camping trip near Friendly Creek.